When Bees Win

by Lisa Galjanic

Illustrations by Michelle Hope

LSG
PUBLICATIONS

1065 Bay Avenue • East Marion, NY • 11939
29165 Clover Lane • Big Pine Key, FL • 33043

When Bees Win

First printing 2007

International Standard Book Number 978-1-933532-04-2

Library of Congress Control Number: 2005905587

ATTENTION CORPORATIONS, SCHOOLS, PROFESSIONAL AND CHARITABLE ORGANIZATIONS:
Quantity discounts are available on bulk purchases of this book for educational and gift purposes, or as premiums for promoting your organization. For information, contact LSG Publications at www.lsgpublications.com.

For Nicholas and John.
There's such a thing as having too much.

Special thanks to Allison Antebi, Michelle Cooper, Joanne Hahn, and
Gloria Walko, without whose talents this book could not have been published.

Other titles by Lisa Galjanic

When Leaves Die

When Fish Are Mean

When Squirrels Try

When Caterpillars Grow Up

When Flowers Dance

For ordering information, visit www.lsgpublications.com

When Bees Win

by Lisa Galjanic

Illustrations by Michelle Hope

One day in a beautiful forest, a family of honeybees made their home in a hollow log under a tall tree.

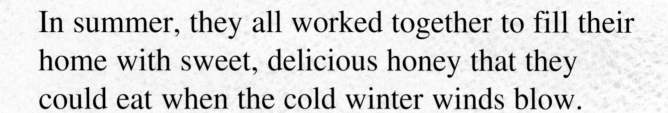

In summer, they all worked together to fill their home with sweet, delicious honey that they could eat when the cold winter winds blow.

The bees felt cozy and safe
inside their beehive home,
and they were happy.

Until ...

…one cold day, just before winter, a hungry bear came to their forest sniffing for something to eat.

The bees watched in fear as the bear
came closer and closer to their beehive.

They knew that a bear's favorite food is sweet, delicious honey – the very same honey they had saved up for themselves.

He would take it all and they would have nothing to eat!

But, what could they do to save their honey? They were so small and the bear was so **BIG**! Surely, there was no way the bees could win against the hungry bear.

As the bear came *closer*
and *closer*,

the bees became
more and *more* afraid.

Then, suddenly, one of the
bees had a wonderful idea!

Why not share their honey with the bear? They had worked hard and had made enough honey for themselves *and* the bear to eat.

15

Share their honey
with the hungry bear?!
No! It couldn't be!

But…then again…maybe…yes!
It just might work!

So, when the big, hungry bear poked his sniffing nose into their beehive, the bees offered him some sweet, delicious honey.

19

At first, the bear was very surprised. He didn't think the honeybees would share their honey with him.

Then, he ate the honey and happily smacked his lips. ***Ummm-mmm!***

The bear thanked the bees for sharing their honey, and they all became great friends.

Once again, the honeybees felt cozy and safe inside their beehive home.

But now they were even happier because they had won for themselves a new friend!

Photo: Mellaphoto@earthlink.net

Lisa Galjanic, *author*

Lisa is the author of six popular picture books for young children. Dubbed the "When…" series because each book title begins with the word "when," the stories use the antics of familiar animals to inspire children to face everyday troubles with heart, smarts, and spunk. A mother of two, Lisa develops her stories from her experiences in helping her children confront tough situations in positive ways. The "When…" books have been selected for New York's Stories and Soundscapes program, where they are set to original scores and performed by professional actors and musicians for children of all ages. Lisa also dramatizes her works in interactive performances at libraries, schools, and private functions. She can be reached at www.lsgpublications.com.

Michelle Hope, *illustrator*

Michelle is a freelance artist who wants to make a difference. Her philosophy is to "just say yes" to life and live your dreams. Her creative style is simple and unique as she tours the United States on her motorcycle admiring the awe-inspiring natural beauty that is so creatively fulfilling for her. Michelle's motorcycle is her traveling art studio where she uses watercolors to paint nature, her favorite subject. As a mother of four grown children, she believes that children are born with a deep understanding of art and creativity, and she hopes that her illustrations will awaken their inner appreciation and natural ability for art.